CARTOON NETWORK™

SCOOBY-DOO!

AND THE

DEEP-SEA DIVER

Look for these recent **Scooby-Doo Mysteries**.
Collect as many as you can!

CARTOON NETWORK

SCOOBY-DOO!

AND THE

DEEP-SEA DIVER

Written by
James Gelsey

WORLDWIDE PUBLISHING

A
LITTLE APPLE
PAPERBACK

SCHOLASTIC INC.

New York Toronto London Auckland Sydney
Mexico City New Delhi Hong Kong Buenos Aires

For Zack and Eric

ISBN 0-439-42073-3

Designed by Carisa Swenson

12 11 10 9 8 7 6 5 4 3 2 1   3 4 5 6 7 8/0

Special thanks to Duendes del Sur for cover and interior illustrations.
Printed in the U.S.A.
First printing, March 2003

Chapter 1

"Ewwww! What's that smell?" Shaggy called from the back of the Mystery Machine. Holding his nose, he poked his head up between Daphne and Velma. "Don't you guys smell that?"

"Shaggy, we're at Skipper Joe's Nautical Museum," Velma said. "And that's the smell of the harbor and all kinds of nautical adventures."

"That smell's going to give me, like, nauseous adventures," Shaggy said.

"Re, roo," Scooby echoed.

"You'll have plenty of time to get used to

1

it, fellas," Daphne said. "We're spending the rest of the afternoon here, remember?"

Shaggy and Scooby looked at each other.

"Like, why would we want to do that?" asked Shaggy.

"To do research for the annual homecoming parade," Daphne said.

"This year the parade has a nautical theme," Fred added. "And we're in charge of one of the floats. So we've come to Skipper Joe's museum to look at the old ships and get some ideas."

"Like, isn't there a less smelly way to do this?" asked Shaggy.

Fred steered the Mystery Machine into a parking space by a large sailing ship. "Here we are, gang," he announced. "Skipper Joe's Nautical Museum."

The gang got out of the van and looked at a large wooden ship docked in front of them. Three large masts towered over the vessel. A web of rigging lines hung from the various

cross beams. The ship itself seemed longer than ten Mystery Machines.

"Rat's a rig roat," Scooby said.

"Aye, but it's not just any boat," a gruff voice said behind them. "That there's the *Zephyr*, one of the finest clipper ships that ever sailed."

The gang turned around and came face-to-face with a grizzled old sea captain. His weathered blue captain's hat barely contained

his frizzled mop of gray hair. His white shirt and faded blue pants looked like they'd seen better days.

"Captain Jonas Q. Forecastle, at your service," he announced, removing his hat. "But you can call me Skipper Joe."

"Nice to meet you, Skipper," Fred said. "I'm Fred. And this is Velma, Daphne, Shaggy, and Scooby-Doo."

Skipper Joe gave each of them a slight nod and a wink. He put his hat back on and took a red bandanna from his back pocket. He blew his nose with a loud HONK that sent the seagulls flying away.

"And what brings you kids down here today?" he asked.

"We want to build a model of a boat for

our school's parade," Daphne explained. "But we want to make sure we do it right. So we've come to take a look at all the historical ships in your museum."

"Aye, the ships." Skipper Joe nodded sadly. "Sorry to say, kids, but they're all gone. All but this one, anyway."

"Why? What happened to them?" asked Fred.

"Most of them were so old, they were falling apart," Skipper Joe said. "So I decided to sell 'em for scrap and use the money to do two things. First I restored this boat right here."

Skipper Joe beamed as he looked at the mighty clipper ship.

"Yes, sir, I rebuilt the *Zephyr* timber by timber," Skipper Joe said. "Took me two years. This clipper ship is the finest example of nautical know-how at its best."

"And what was the second thing you did with the money?" asked Daphne.

"Something very special." Skipper Joe winked at the gang.

"Like, build a snack bar?" asked Shaggy.

"Even better," Skipper Joe said. "Bought Captain Phineas Tarwhistle's hat."

"What's the big deal about a hat?" asked Shaggy.

"Shaggy, Captain Tarwhistle is one of the most famous sea captains ever," Velma said.

"That's right, Velma," Skipper Joe said.

"But he disappeared one day, never to be heard from again."

"Isn't there a legend that he buried treasure somewhere?" Fred asked.

"Aye, Fred, somewhere around here." Skipper Joe nodded. "They say he kept the treasure map in his hat."

"So why don't you just take the map out and get the treasure?" Shaggy asked.

Skipper Joe leaned closer to the gang. "Because of the curse," he whispered.

Shaggy and Scooby jumped back.

"Rurse?" Scooby asked.

"Okay, Scooby and I have heard enough," Shaggy said. "We'd love to stick around with, like, the smells and the curse and everything, but we have to go."

"Oh, no you don't," Velma said. "We're not going to let a little curse scare us away. We came here to look at some ships and that's what we're going to do."

"Besides, fellas, I hear there's a great restaurant on the other side of the dock," Daphne added.

"Aye, Daphne, 'tis true," Skipper Joe said. "They've got the best banana splits in all the seven seas."

"There you go, Shaggy," Fred said. "What more could you ask for?"

Chapter 2

As the gang followed Skipper Joe along the dock, they passed a row of old-fashioned deep-sea diving suits and gear. The round metal helmets each had a circular window in the middle. The puffy suits were propped up against wooden frames.

"Are these diving suits part of the museum, too?" asked Daphne.

"Aye," Skipper Joe replied. "They used to belong to Monsoon Max, and they're all in perfect working condition. Monsoon Max used the suits to dive for treasures lost at the bottom of the sea. They say he even went after Captain Tarwhistle's treasure."

"Did he find it?" asked Fred.

"Let's just say that he went down but never came back up," Skipper Joe said.

Shaggy and Scooby stopped in front of the last diving suit.

"Man, the only way you'd get me into one of those things is to go deep-dish-pizza diving," Shaggy said with a chuckle.

Skipper Joe led the gang up a narrow walkway and onto the deck of the ship. "Welcome aboard the *Zephyr*," he announced. "The finest clipper ship ever built."

"Skipper Joe, why did they call them clipper ships?" asked Daphne.

"Because they traveled faster than any other ship in their day," Skipper Joe said. "They sailed, as they say, at a good clip."

"That, and because anyone who ended up working on one felt like he had his wings clipped," said a man holding a mop. "No shore leave, no down-time, not even the chance to stand behind the wheel and pretend to drive."

"How many times do I have to tell you, Monty, that you don't drive a ship?" asked Skipper Joe. "You captain a ship. You guide a ship. You can steer or rudder a ship. But you can't drive a ship!"

Monty, the man with the mop, frowned and stared down at the deck. "Sorry, Skipper," he said.

Skipper Joe walked over to Monty and put his hand on the young man's shoulder. "That's all right, me boy," said Skipper Joe. "You'll get the hang of it soon. One day, you'll be a mighty fine captain. Just not today. Now finish swabbing the deck. We've got company."

He gave Monty a hearty slap on the back and turned back to the gang.

"You kids wait here," he said. "I've got something to show ya."

Skipper Joe disappeared through a door that led belowdecks. After checking that the captain was safely out of earshot, Monty threw down the mop.

"Boy, he really churns my butter!" Monty exclaimed.

"What's the matter, Monty?" asked Daphne.

"I spent the past two years helping him rebuild this ship for his museum and I'm still mopping the deck," Monty complained. "The only reason I started working with him was to learn to be a real sea captain. Look, I've even been studying in my free time."

Monty reached over and yanked the cushion off of a wooden bench. He lifted up the bench's lid and pulled out a thick stack of papers.

"These are maps and charts of the oceans, all the major seas, and even this dinky little harbor here," Monty said. "I've memorized every nook and cranny, every jetty and sand-bar, every latitude and longitude."

"Seems to me that all you need now is, like, a boat," Shaggy said.

"Shaggy!" scolded Daphne.

"No, he's right." Monty sighed. He put the

13

papers back into the bench. "I need a ship of my own. Or at least the money to buy one. And I have no idea where I'm ever going to find enough money to buy my own boat."

At that moment, Skipper Joe bounded back on deck carrying a metal box.

"Here 'tis!" he announced. "One of the most valuable — and cursed — objects in all the seven seas. Feast yer eyes."

He opened the metal box. Everyone peered inside.

"That beat-up blue hat is Captain Tar-whistle's famous hat?" asked Fred.

"None other, me boy," Skipper Joe replied proudly.

"Wow!" gasped Monty. "Captain Phineas Tarwhistle's hat!"

"Monty, didn't I tell you to finish swabbing the deck?" asked Skipper Joe.

"Aye, aye, captain," Monty said. He grabbed his mop and went back to work.

"I've already started spreading the word," Skipper Joe said. "This hat will attract the tourists like seagulls to a garbage scow."

"So far, he's got the smell right," Shaggy whispered to Scooby.

Chapter 3

"Now then, kids, why don't you take a look around while I put this back below-decks," Skipper Joe said.

"Great," Shaggy said. "Where's the kitchen?"

"Not kitchen," Velma said. "On a ship it's called the galley. Besides, I don't think they actually serve food there anymore. This is a museum, remember?"

"Then how about we go check out the front of the boat, Scooby?" asked Shaggy.

"No, Shaggy, bow," Fred said.

Shaggy looked at Scooby and shrugged

his shoulders. "If you say so, Fred-o." Shaggy and Scooby stood up tall and then bowed to Fred, Daphne, and Velma.

"What are you two doing?" asked Velma.

"Bowing, of course," Shaggy said. "Like Fred just said."

"I didn't tell you to bow," Fred said.

"Sure you did," Shaggy replied. "I said we wanted to see the front of the ship and you told us to bow."

"No, Shaggy, I meant that the front of a ship is called the bow," Fred said.

Shaggy looked at Scooby.

"Ruh?" Scooby said.

"Ahoy!" a voice called from the dock. "I say, ahoy there!"

The gang looked around but didn't see any sign of Skipper Joe or Monty. Fred walked over to the side of the ship and looked down at the dock. A man in shorts, a T-shirt, flip-flops, and a floppy straw hat was studying the row of diving suits and gear. He looked up and saw Fred.

"Is this Skipper Joe's Nautical Museum?" he called.

"Yes," Fred replied. "Come on up."

The man made his way up the narrow walkway and met the others at the top of the ramp.

"Pip Penrod's the name," the man said as he tossed his bag onto the deck. "I'm looking for Skipper Joe."

"He'll be right back," Daphne said.

Pip Penrod walked across the deck and climbed up on the ship's railing. He looked out over the harbor in all directions. Skipper Joe came back on deck and saw the man up there.

"Are you crazy, man?" yelled Skipper Joe. "Climb on down here before you fall!"

The man turned and jumped into the air. He did a double flip and landed with both feet on the deck.

"If you're looking for the gymnastics museum, you're in the wrong place, sonny," Skipper Joe growled.

"Pip Penrod's the name, Skipper," Pip said, extending his hand.

"Arr, Pip Penrod," Skipper Joe said. "You're the scalawag that kept bidding me up on the hat."

Pip noticed the puzzled look on Fred's, Daphne's, and Velma's faces.

"Skipper Joe and I were in a bidding war for Captain Tarwhistle's hat," he explained. "I lost."

"Then why are you here, Mr. Penrod?" Fred asked.

"To get a glimpse of it," Pip said. "And to

make Skipper Joe an offer." Pip Penrod grabbed his bag and opened it up.

"Jinkies, look at all that diving equipment," Velma said. "There's an underwater camera and flashlight."

"And maps and everything else we'll need, Skipper," Pip said.

"For what?" Skipper Joe asked suspiciously.

"For finding Captain Tarwhistle's treasure,"

Pip said. "Now that you have the hat, you have the map."

"What's this?" asked Shaggy, picking up a rectangular object wrapped in aluminum foil.

"A spinach-and-tomato sandwich," Pip replied, grabbing the sandwich from Shaggy. "For my lunch."

"Now see here, Penrod," Skipper Joe said. "No one's looking for any treasure as long as I've got that hat. No sir, I'm not going to let the curse of Captain Tarwhistle get the better of me. Now get your gear off of my boat before I make you walk the plank."

"Have it your way, Skipper. For now," Pip Penrod said as he put his equipment away.

"Come on, kids, let's go astern and I'll show you around," Skipper Joe said.

Before Shaggy could ask what that was, Velma said, "The back of the boat."

"Galley, bow, stern. The next time I go on a boat, Scooby, remind me to bring a dictionary," Shaggy said.

Chapter 4

The gang followed Skipper Joe to the rear of the boat. On their way, they passed two of the *Zephyr*'s mighty masts.

"Jinkies!" Velma exclaimed. "I never realized how tall the masts were on a ship this size."

"Aye, Velma," Skipper Joe said. "Mighty they are. But you haven't seen anything until you've seen them fully rigged with every last sail, from the outer jib to the mizzen royal."

"There he goes with those funny words again," Shaggy whispered to Scooby.

Skipper Joe stopped at the very rear of the ship and pointed to the railing.

"If you look down there, you'll see the *Zephyr's* rudder," he said. "It was so crusted with barnacles I had to strip the thing down to the bare nubbins and build it back up again. And I used real gold paint for the letters in *Zephyr*."

Everyone looked over the railing.

"Golly, that's very impressive, Skipper Joe," Daphne said.

Skipper Joe tipped his hat. "That's mighty kind, Daphne," he said.

"Skipper Joe, I think, like, the boat's burping," Shaggy said.

"What's that, lad?" asked Skipper Joe.

"There's a bunch of bubbles coming up from under the boat," Shaggy said.

Fred looked over the rail again. "Shaggy's right," he said. "Only I don't think the boat's burping. It looks like a —"

"Sea monster? The ghost of Monsoon Max? I knew it! Let's go, Scooby!" Shaggy cried.

"It looks like a scuba diver," Velma said, peering over the rail. A moment later, someone in a yellow scuba diving suit surfaced next to the rudder. The diver looked up at the gang and waved.

"Well, shiver me timbers, if it isn't Dr. Kelp," Skipper Joe said. "Come on up here, Doc."

The gang watched as the diver swam around to a ladder hanging off the side of the

ship. The diver climbed up the ladder and over the railing.

"This is my old friend Dr. Kelp," Skipper Joe said as he helped the diver take off his air tank. Dr. Kelp removed the scuba suit's mouthpiece and face mask.

"Nice to meet you, sir," Daphne said.

Dr. Kelp peeled off the scuba headpiece and shook his head. Blond hair tumbled down around his shoulders.

"Zoinks!" Shaggy exclaimed. "He's a she!"

"Hi there, kids, I'm Harriet Kelp," the diver said with a great big smile on her face.

"What brings you out to these waters, Dr. Kelp?" asked Skipper Joe.

"This!" she answered, holding out a handful of slimy green leaves.

Shaggy jumped into Scooby's arms.

"Look out, Scooby, it's the attack of the killer slime!" Shaggy screamed.

"No more late-night television for you two," Velma said. "It's just seaweed."

Dr. Kelp smiled. "It is seaweed, but not *just* seaweed," she explained. "It's a special kind of seaweed that can only be found around here. It has a lot of nutrients that are good for people. I've been studying maps of the area to see if there are any unusual environmental influences that make the seaweed so special. I'm hoping to open a seaweed lab right here on the dock."

"Sounds fascinating, Dr. Kelp," Velma said.

Dr. Kelp's smile faded away as she put the seaweed into a plastic bag. She unzipped a pouch hanging from her dive belt and put the seaweed bag inside.

"Only problem is that my funding fell through," she said. "I wish there was some way I could find the money to finish my research and let the whole world know about the seaweed here."

"Aye, in time, Dr. Kelp, in time," Skipper Joe said.

"But enough about me," Dr. Kelp said. "Did you get the hat, Jonas?"

Skipper Joe smiled at her and nodded.

"I'm going to go back to my car to get my clothes," Dr. Kelp said. "When I get back, I want to see that hat!"

Dr. Kelp grabbed her scuba gear and walked off the boat.

"Aye, I'd better go get the hat so Dr. Kelp can see it," Skipper Joe said. "I'll be back in two shakes of a crab's claw." Skipper Joe scuttled across the deck and down the stairs.

Chapter 5

"While we're waiting for Skipper Joe to come back, I'm going to make some sketches we can bring home with us," Daphne said. She took a pencil and a small notebook from her pocket. The gang walked toward the front of the ship. The deck became narrower and narrower until it tapered to a point.

"Hey! It looks like someone forgot to let go when they walked the plank," Shaggy said. He pointed to a long, thick piece of wood that extended out over the bow of the ship.

The wooden figure of a person was carved into the wood.

"That's not the plank, young man," Skipper Joe said, holding the metal box with Captain Tarwhistle's hat. "That piece of wood's called the bowsprit. And that person is Zephyrus, the god of the west wind from old mythology."

"O-O-O-O-O-O-O-O-O-O-O-O-O!"

"Like, knock it off, Scooby," Shaggy said. "That's the creepiest imitation of the west wind I've ever heard."

"Rasn't re," Scooby said.

"Well, if it wasn't you, who was it?" asked Daphne.

"O-O-O-O-O-O-O-O-O-O-O-O-O-O!"

Everyone turned around.

"Zoinks!" Shaggy cried.

"Jinkies!" Velma exclaimed.

"Arr! 'Tis the ghost of Monsoon Max!" Skipper Joe shouted.

Monsoon Max's deep-sea diving suit stood before the gang. It dripped with water and seaweed. The diver howled again.

"O-O-O-O-O-O! Give me the treasure!" he moaned.

"What treasure?" asked Skipper Joe.

The deep-sea diver raised his arm and pointed at the metal box in Skipper Joe's hand.

"No! You can't have it!" Skipper Joe replied.

"I must have the treasure!" the diver shouted. Then he tossed a giant fishing net through the air. The net landed right on top of Skipper Joe and the gang.

"Hey! What's the big idea?" Fred shouted. While everyone struggled under the net, the diver walked over and cut a small hole in it. He reached in and yanked the metal box from Skipper Joe's hand.

"Noooo!" shouted Skipper Joe. "Give me that box!"

The diver opened the box and took out Captain Tarwhistle's faded blue captain's hat. As he threw the metal box to the deck, Daphne wriggled out from under the net. But before she could get away, the diver grabbed her wrist.

"Let me go!" she yelled.

"Hahahahahahahaha," the diver cackled as he dragged Daphne away. "The treasure is mine! The treasure is mine!" He pulled Daphne toward the back of the ship.

"Come on, gang! We have to help Daphne!" Fred said. Everyone struggled to get untangled.

"Hold it, mateys," ordered Skipper Joe. "We'll never get out of here if we keep flopping around like fish out of water." With everyone still, Skipper Joe found the small hole made by the diver. He and Fred grabbed the net and ripped it apart, making an opening large enough for everyone.

"Let's go!" Fred said. They followed the diver's trail of water and seaweed across the deck and down the narrow gangway to the dock.

"Keep your eyes open for anything unusual, Shaggy," Fred said.

"You mean like a burping boat?" asked Shaggy.

"Where?" asked Fred.

"Rere!" Scooby barked.

Everyone watched as a trail of air bubbles disappeared below the water's surface.

"Jinkies!" Velma exclaimed. "Monsoon Max has gone back into the water and taken Daphne with him!"

Chapter 6

"How long do you think Daphne can hold her breath?" asked Shaggy.

"I have a hunch she's not holding her breath, Shaggy," Velma said.

"How do you know that?" Shaggy said.

"Because two diving suits are missing," Velma said. "See?"

Everyone looked at the row of diving suits. Sure enough, there were two empty spaces in the line of diving suits.

"Monsoon Max must be using his old suit," Fred said. "And that means Daphne must have taken the other one."

"I just hope there's enough air in the tanks," Velma said.

"Aye, Velma, don't worry," Skipper Joe said. "Like I said before, those suits are in perfect condition, just in case some hearty tourists want to go for a dive."

"They may have air, but it looks like they left something else behind," Velma said. She walked over and picked up a piece of paper from the dock. Fred and Skipper Joe took a look at it, too.

"Why, that's part of a nautical chart," Skipper Joe said. "Looks to me like a chart of this very part of the harbor."

"Great find, Velma," Fred said. "This clue is our first step to solving the mystery. But if we're going to find Daphne, we have to act quickly. Shaggy, Scooby, how do you feel about going for a swim?"

"Gee, Fred, I'd love to, but I'm, like, allergic to water," Shaggy said.

"Rot re," Scooby said.

"That's the spirit, Scooby," Velma said. "See, Shaggy, Scooby understands how important it is to help find Daphne."

"All right, Scoob," Shaggy said. "I'll go, too."

"I'll help you lads into your suits," Skipper Joe said.

"And Velma and I will look around for more clues," Fred said. "Let's meet back on deck as soon as possible."

Fred and Velma examined the dock on their way back to the

ship. Skipper Joe grabbed the remaining two diving suits and brought them over to Shaggy and Scooby.

"Nothing to it, boys," Skipper Joe said. "Like putting on pajamas."

Shaggy struggled into his diving suit.

"You mean, like, cement pajamas," he said. "These things weigh a ton."

"On land maybe," Skipper Joe said. "But once you're underwater, it'll be like floating on a cloud."

After Shaggy and Scooby were suited up, Skipper Joe placed the round metal helmets over their heads. He opened up the little glass windows in front of their faces.

"Now then, lads," he said. "You've each got a full tank of air. Just breathe normally and take your time down there. Here's an underwater flashlight. Any questions?"

"Yeah," Shaggy said. "Like, how did I let you talk me into this, Scooby?"

Skipper Joe closed the little windows and made sure the suits were tightly sealed. He led

Shaggy and Scooby to the edge of the dock and pushed them into the water at the same time.

Shaggy and Scooby slowly sank beneath the water's surface. Farther and farther down they went until they hit the sandy bottom of the harbor. Shaggy turned on the flashlight.

Aside from some rocks and some garbage, there wasn't much to see. Shaggy and Scooby looked up and saw the *Zephyr* floating above

them. They swim-walked along the bottom, shining the flashlight ahead of them.

Something caught Shaggy's eye on a rock up ahead. They swam over and found an underwater camera. Just as Shaggy picked it up, Scooby saw something moving in the water. Scooby tapped Shaggy on the shoulder. Shaggy looked up, following Scooby's gaze.

Monsoon Max was swimming after them!

Chapter 7

S haggy and Scooby swam to the surface as fast as they could. Each time Shaggy looked down behind him, he saw the diver getting closer. Scooby found the ladder on the side of the ship. He climbed out with Shaggy right behind him.

Back onboard the *Zephyr,* they shouted things to each other, but neither of them could hear with their helmets on. Shaggy opened his tiny little window.

"Run, Scooby!" he shouted. But the suits were so heavy, neither of them could move. Shaggy reached up and managed to take off his helmet. He helped Scooby take off his, and then they both scrambled out of their diving suits.

"He's gonna be here any minute, Scooby," Shaggy cried. "We've got to hide!"

They ran along the deck of the ship. Shaggy spied a cushioned bench and remembered that Monty kept things in one of them.

"In here, Scooby!" Shaggy said. He tossed the cushion off the bench and lifted up the bench cover. Out popped Daphne.

"Aaaaahhhhhh!" Shaggy cried as he jumped back. "Like, don't ever scare me like that again, Daphne!"

"Raphne!" Scooby barked. He licked her face.

"Hi, Scooby," Daphne laughed between licks. "Thanks for finding me, Shaggy."

"Move over, Daph, that diving demon is after us!" Shaggy said.

"What diving demon?" asked Velma from behind them.

"Aaaaaaah!" Shaggy jumped into Scooby's arms. "Stop scaring me! Like, what is it with you people?"

"Daphne!" Fred said. "You're all right!"

"And you're dry," Velma added.

"We thought that Monsoon Max took you underwater with him," Fred said.

"No, right after he grabbed me, he dragged me to the back of the boat and put me in here," Daphne said. "I don't know what happened after that."

As Skipper Joe came over, he stepped over the pile of diving suits that Shaggy and Scooby left behind. He noticed the camera there and picked it up.

"Looks like you found something down there," Skipper Joe said.

"We found something, all right," Shaggy said. "We found that spooky sea diver. He chased us all the way back to the ship."

"I think Skipper Joe means the camera, Shaggy," Daphne said.

"Oh, yeah, we found that, too," Shaggy added.

Velma and Fred looked at the camera closely.

"This is no ordinary camera," Fred said. "It's specially designed for underwater photography."

"That's an odd thing to find," Daphne said.

"Not if someone dropped it while searching for something underwater," Fred said.

"Here's something even stranger about it," Velma said. She reached over and picked a slimy green leaf off the camera.

"That's just more of the seaweed that Dr. Kelp was going crazy about," Skipper Joe said.

"I'm not so sure," Velma said. "This may be green, but it's not seaweed. It looks like another kind of green leaf."

Fred and Daphne took a closer look and nodded.

"I think Velma's on to something," Daphne said.

"You know what that means, gang," Fred said. "It's time to set a trap!"

Chapter 8

"Arr, you'll need a special kind of trap to catch Monsoon Max," Skipper Joe said.

"That's why I've got a special kind of plan," Fred replied. "And I'll need a special volunteer for the most important part."

Scooby-Doo jumped behind Shaggy and lifted Shaggy's arm into the air.

"Rike, ri'll ro rit," Scooby said in his best Shaggy voice.

"Scooby, it's not very nice to volunteer other people," Daphne said.

"Like, thanks, Daph," Shaggy said. "Man,

for a minute there I thought I was going to be Fred's special volunteer."

"Don't worry, Shaggy," Fred said. "You won't have to do it — alone, that is. Scooby will help."

"Nice going, Scoob," Shaggy said to his pal.

"Rorry," Scooby replied.

"We're running out of time," Velma said. "We have to catch Monsoon Max before he finds the treasure."

"Right, so here's the plan," Fred began. "Shaggy and Scooby, you'll go back into the water to find the deep-sea diver. Get him to chase you back onto the ship. When he does, Daphne and Velma will be hiding in the benches around the deck. As the diver chases Shaggy and Scooby, the two of you will jump out and surprise him. That's when Skipper Joe and I will capture Monsoon Max with the fishing net."

"Sounds simple enough," Shaggy said. "Except for one thing."

"What's that?" asked Daphne.

"I think Scooby would rather walk the plank than get chased by that freaky diver again," Shaggy answered.

Everyone looked over and saw Scooby standing on a narrow plank that extended out over the water.

"Come on down, Scooby," Velma called. "It won't be that bad."

"Ruh-uh," Scooby said, taking a step farther out along the plank.

"If you come back and help us, we'll give you a Scooby Snack," Daphne said.

Scooby thought for a moment, but then shook his head.

"Two Scooby Snacks?" Daphne said.

"Roh roy!" Scooby barked. He jumped off the plank and back onto the deck of the ship. Daphne took two Scooby Snacks from her pocket and tossed them into the air. Scooby ate them both in a flash.

"Now that we've got that settled, let's get going," Fred said. "Velma, you and Daphne get into position. Skipper Joe, can you get Shaggy and Scooby ready again?"

"Aye, aye, Fred," Skipper Joe said.

Just as everyone turned to go, they heard a familiar sound.

"O-O-O-O-O-O!"

"D-d-did you hear that?" Shaggy gulped. "Th-th-that sounded like . . . like . . ."

Everyone looked up and saw the deep-sea diver standing on the plank.

"Monsoon Max!" everyone cried.

The diver jumped off the plank and onto the deck of the ship. Fred and Velma ran in one direction, and Skipper Joe and Daphne ran in the other. Shaggy and Scooby watched as the diver walked toward them.

"Run on the count of three, Scoob," Shaggy whispered. "One . . . two . . . three!"

The diver reached out to grab Scooby, but he ducked out of the way just in time and scrambled up one of the tall masts. Shaggy jumped to his right and fell over a big coil of rope. The deep-sea diver slowly walked toward Shaggy.

"Zoinks!" Shaggy cried. "Help! Scooby!" Shaggy crawled backward along the deck as the deep-sea diver slowly approached. Shaggy bumped into the side of the ship. The diver stepped over one edge of

the rope and stopped with both of his feet in-side the coil.

"Rold on, Raggy!" Scooby yelled from the mast pole. Scooby grabbed onto one of the ropes hanging alongside the mast. His weight pulled the rope down, and Scooby swung down it to the deck. As he did, the rope around the diver's feet started flying up into the air.

"Look! Scooby's raising one of the sails!" Daphne called.

Fred, Daphne, Velma, and Skipper Joe ran over and pulled faster and faster on Scooby's rope. The next thing the diver knew, the rope tightened around his feet and whipped him up into the air. Monsoon Max swung upside down ten feet above the deck.

Chapter 9

"All right, mateys, careful now," Skipper Joe said. "Easy does it."

Fred, Shaggy, Velma, Daphne, and Scooby slowly lowered the deep-sea diver down onto the deck. Skipper Joe quickly tied the diver's hands behind his back.

"Are you ready to see who's really behind this mystery?" Fred asked.

"Aye, Fred," Skipper Joe said. He unfastened the big metal helmet and lifted it off the diver's shoulders.

"Well, shiver me timbers, it's that sea scum Pip Penrod," Skipper Joe said.

"Just as we thought," Daphne said.

"Arr, now how in the name of King Neptune himself did you kids know that?" asked Skipper Joe.

"We just put together the clues we found," Velma said. "Like the piece of that ocean chart we found first."

"It looked like one of the charts that your first mate, Monty, showed us," Fred said.

"So that made Monty our first suspect," Fred continued. "Then we remembered that

Pip Penrod and Dr. Kelp also had similar charts with them. That's when we knew the diver had to be one of those three suspects."

Skipper Joe squinted his eyes and slowly nodded as he listened.

"Then Shaggy and Scooby found the underwater camera, just before they found me," Daphne said. "And we realized that both Dr. Kelp and Mr. Penrod had brought one with them for their underwater work. So that eliminated Monty."

"Where is Monty anyway?" Skipper Joe asked.

"Oops!" Shaggy said. "Like, he gave us this note to give to you, but in all the excitement, we forgot."

Shaggy handed Skipper Joe a folded piece of paper. Skipper Joe read it and smiled.

"Seems the lad had to go to the pharmacy," Skipper Joe said. "Needed some medicine for his seasickness."

"But it wasn't until we found the last clue that we figured the whole thing out," Velma said.

"You mean that piece of seaweed?" asked Shaggy.

"It looked like seaweed, all right," Fred said. "But it wasn't. It was another kind of soggy green leaf. Spinach!"

"Spinach!" Skipper Joe exclaimed. "I didn't know you could find spinach growing under the water."

"You can't," Daphne said. "But you can find it on a spinach-and-tomato sandwich."

"Like the one Pip Penrod brought along for his lunch," Shaggy added.

"That's right, Shaggy," Daphne said. "How'd you remember that?"

"I never forget a sandwich," Shaggy said proudly.

"I knew I should have brought peanut-butter-and-jelly instead," Pip muttered angrily. "Everything was going perfectly. I was this close to find-

ing that treasure. I was going to be rich, rich, I tell you. But then you kids showed up and ruined everything. You and that deep-sea-diving dog of yours."

"Arr, Pip Penrod, you truly are the lowest of the low," Skipper Joe said. "Now, where's me hat?"

"Don't you mean Captain Tarwhistle's hat?" asked Daphne.

"No, I mean mine," Skipper Joe said. "I didn't want to take any chances, so I switched my hat with Captain Tarwhistle's. They

looked alike, and that way I could keep the
real treasure map close to me. I put a phony
map in my hat."

"You mean I went through all this trouble
for a worthless map and your smelly old hat?"
Pip Penrod exclaimed. "I can't believe it!"

"Believe it," Skipper Joe said.

"So now that we know there really isn't a curse on the map," Fred said, "what are you going to do with the treasure, Skipper Joe?"

"Oh, I'm not going to look for the treasure," Skipper Joe said. "It belongs to the sea now. But I would like to thank you kids somehow. And especially that wonderful dog of yours."

Scooby ran over to Skipper Joe, who put his captain's hat on Scooby's head.

"Three cheers for Scooby-Doo," Shaggy said.

"That's Skipper Scooby to you," Skipper Joe said.

"Scooby-Dooby-Doo!" barked Scooby.